First edition for the United States published 1995 by
Barron's Educational Series, Inc.

First published in Great Britain by HarperCollins Publishers Ltd in 1994
77-85 Fulham Palace Road, Hammersmith, London W6 8JB.

Text and illustrations copyright © Tim Vyner 1994

All inquiries should be addressed to:
Barron's Educational Series, Inc.
250 Wireless Boulevard
Hauppauge, New York 11788

Library of Congress Card No.: 94-30417
International Standard Book No. 0-8120-9170-1 (paperback)
0-8120-6492-5 (hardcover)
Printed in Hong Kong
5678   9934   98765432

THE TREE
IN THE FOREST

Tim Vyner

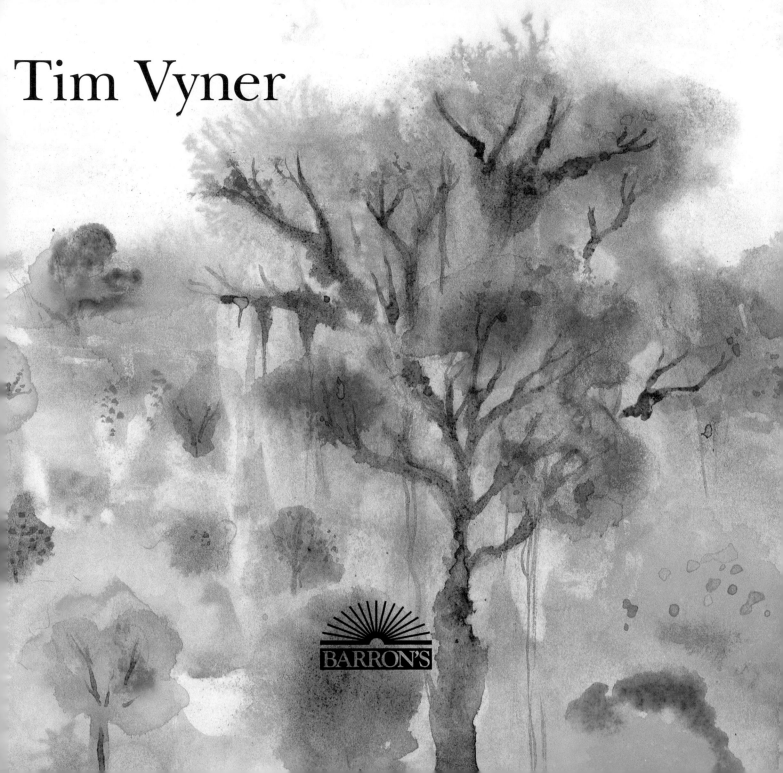

BARRON'S

This is the tree
that grew in the heart of the forest.

On a leaf is the frog
who sang in the tree
that grew in the heart of the forest.

This is the snake
that searched for the frog
who sang in the tree
that grew in the heart of the forest.

On a branch swings the monkey
who missed the snake
that searched for the frog
who sang in the tree
that grew in the heart of the forest.

Here is the cat that leaps and pounces,
that chased the monkey who swung from a branch,
who missed the snake
that searched for the frog
who sang in the tree
that grew in the heart of the forest.

The three-toed sloth hangs silent and still,
who fooled the cat that leaped and pounced,
that chased the monkey who swung from a branch,
who missed the snake
that searched for the frog
who sang in the tree
that grew in the heart of the forest.

The racing tamarins who run with great skill,
jumped past the sloth hanging silent and still,
who fooled the cat that leaped and pounced,
that chased the monkey who swung from a branch,
who missed the snake
that searched for the frog
who sang in the tree
that grew in the heart of the forest.

The hungry panther, stalking a kill,
prowled under the tamarins who run with great skill,
that jumped past the sloth hanging silent and still,
who fooled the cat that leaped and pounced,
that chased the monkey who swung from a branch,
who missed the snake
that searched for the frog
who sang in the tree
that grew in the heart of the forest.

In the canopy a toucan, colorful and bright,
spotted the panther stalking a kill,
who prowled under the tamarins who run with great skill,
that jumped past the sloth hanging silent and still,
who fooled the cat that leaped and pounced,
that chased the monkey who swung from a branch,
who missed the snake
that searched for the frog
who sang in the tree
that grew in the heart of the forest.

The jewel-like beetle frozen with fright,
escaped from the toucan, colorful and bright,
that spotted the panther stalking a kill,
who prowled under the tamarins who run with great skill,
that jumped past the sloth hanging silent and still,
who fooled the cat that leaped and pounced,
that chased the monkey who swung from a branch,
who missed the snake
that searched for the frog
who sang in the tree
that grew in the heart of the forest.

This is the seed which fell from a height,
that hit the beetle frozen with fright,
who escaped from the toucan, colorful and bright,
that spotted the panther stalking a kill,
who prowled under the tamarins who run with great skill,
that jumped past the sloth hanging silent and still,
who fooled the cat that leaped and pounced,
that chased the monkey who swung from a branch,
who missed the snake
that searched for the frog
who sang in the tree
that grew in the heart of the forest.

This is the sapling standing upright,
  that grew from the seed which fell from a height,
that hit the beetle frozen with fright,
who escaped from the toucan, colorful and bright,
that spotted the panther stalking a kill,
who prowled under the tamarins who run with great skill,
that jumped past the sloth hanging silent and still,
who fooled the cat that leaped and pounced,
that chased the monkey who swung from a branch,
who missed the snake
that searched for the frog
who sang in the tree
that grew in the heart of the forest.

TOUCAN

The toucan's brightly colored bill needs to be very light because of its size. It is made of honeycomb-shaped bone, which makes it very strong. This helps the toucan crush hard fruits and unsuspecting insects.

BEETLE

There are more than 250,000 known species of beetle. They come in all shapes and sizes and they provide a rich source of food for many of the other animals in the forest. Beetles avoid being caught by camouflage or by tasting awful. Some have markings that confuse hunters. New species of beetles are still being discovered.

TAMARIN

Emperor tamarins get their name from their whiskers, which look like an old Chinese emperor's mustache. Tamarins are small and light, which means they are fast and agile in the branches. Their tails are longer than the whole length of their bodies.

FROG

Some tree frogs are very poisonous. Amazonian Indians use their poison to make arrows to hunt with, which is why these frogs are sometimes called poison dart frogs. Their bright colors are a warning to other animals that they wouldn't taste very nice! They are very small frogs, less than 2 inches (5 cm) long.

SNAKE

Vine snakes have very thin bodies that can reach out a long way from a branch or a leaf. This allows them to surprise frogs and lizards. They can measure over 3½ feet (1 m) long, but their bodies are not much thicker than a pen.